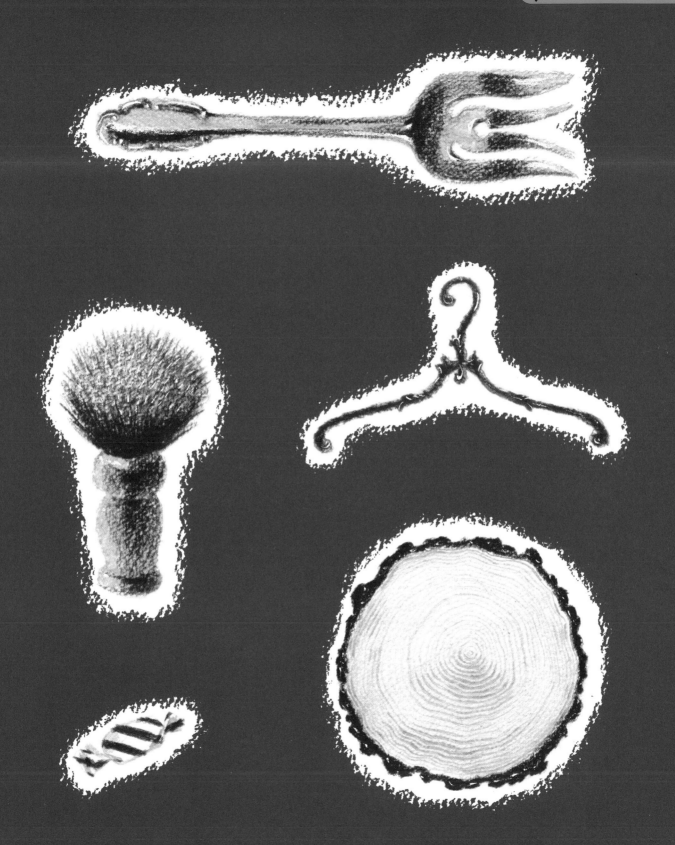

The Tea Party in the Woods

Akiko Miyakoshi

Kids Can Press

THAT MORNING, Kikko had awoken to a winter wonderland.
It had snowed all night.
Now her father was off to Grandma's house to help clear the walk.

"Is this the pie for Grandma?" Kikko asked her mother, spotting the box near the door.

"Oh, dear," her mother said. "Your father forgot it."

"I can still catch up to him," said Kikko.

"All right, but hurry."

Grandma's house was on the other side of the woods.
Kikko set out, following her father's tracks in the fresh snow.
The woods were very still. And so quiet. Kikko's footsteps were the only sound.

After a while, Kikko spied a figure up
ahead in a long coat and a hat.
"Papa!" she called as she ran to catch up.

She struggled in the deep snow and fell.
The pie box was crushed.
Kikko felt like crying. But her father was almost out
of sight. So she picked up the box and hurried after him.

Kikko followed her father all the way to a strange house.
Has it always been here? Kikko wondered. She couldn't
remember having seen it before.

She watched as her father went inside.

Curious, Kikko peered through the window.
She watched as he took off his long coat and hat.
But — he wasn't her father at all!
Kikko had been following a great big bear!

"Are you here for the tea party?" asked a kind voice.
Kikko turned to see a little lamb standing nearby.
"This way," said the lamb, gently taking Kikko's hand and leading her inside.

Kikko couldn't believe her eyes!
And what did the other animals say when they saw her?

"Welcome!" they cheered. A small rabbit led Kikko to her seat.

"You must be cold," said a boar. "Please, come in and warm yourself."

"We're about to serve the tea," said the rabbit. "You're just in time."

Once everyone was seated, a doe stood and began to speak.
"Thank you all for coming on this cold winter day. We have a
special guest with us. What is your name, my dear?"

Kikko's heart raced. She gathered up all her courage and said, "My name is Kikko. I was bringing a pie to Grandma."

The animals all began to speak excitedly.

"That's so brave of you, going all by yourself!"

"Your grandmother will be so pleased."

"Please, have something to eat."

Everyone wanted to talk to the special guest. Kikko began to feel a bit braver.

Over the noise, one of the rabbits spoke up. "Is this the pie for your grandmother?"

Kikko looked down at the crushed box. "Yes, but I fell. And now it's ruined."

The animals glanced at one another.

"If it's pie you need, we have plenty to share!"
Slice by slice, they assembled a new pie on a pretty plate. Each piece had a different filling of seeds and nuts and fruit and other delicious things gathered from the woods.

The doe carefully placed the plate into a new box
and tied it with a red ribbon.

"How nice!" said Kikko. She was so excited that
she wanted to take the pie to Grandma at once.

"We'll come, too!" said the animals.

The woods were filled with joyful sounds as everyone paraded to
Grandma's house, singing and laughing and playing music as they went.
    "This way!" the animals called.
    Kikko held the pie box tightly and walked on.

At last, they reached Grandma's house.
"Go on," the animals encouraged Kikko.

Kikko knocked on the door and called, "Grandma! I've brought you a pie!"

Grandma and Kikko's father appeared at the door, surprised. Kikko handed them the box.

"My dear, did you come all this way on your own?" asked Grandma, stepping inside.

Kikko looked around, but the animals were
nowhere to be seen.

"You're never alone in the woods," Kikko
answered, smiling.

She was sure her new friends were listening.

Originally published in Japanese under the title *Mori no Oku no Ochakai e* by Kaisei-Sha Publishing Co. Ltd.

English translation rights arranged through Japan Foreign-Rights Centre

Kids Can Press acknowledges the financial support of the Government of Ontario, through the Ontario Media Development Corporation's Ontario Book Initiative.

Published in Canada by
Kids Can Press Ltd.
25 Dockside Drive
Toronto, ON M5A 0B5

Published in the U.S. by
Kids Can Press Ltd.
2250 Military Road
Tonawanda, NY 14150

www.kidscanpress.com

English edition edited by Katie Scott and Yvette Ghione.

The artwork in this book was rendered in charcoal, pencil and color ink.

This book is smyth sewn casebound.
Manufactured in Shenzhen, China, in 3/2015 by C & C Offset.

CM 15 0 9 8 7 6 5 4 3 2 1

Library and Archives Canada Cataloguing in Publication

Miyakoshi, Akiko, 1982–
    [Mori no oku no ochakai e. English]
    The tea party in the woods / Akiko Miyakoshi.

Translation of: Mori no oku no ochakai e.
ISBN 978-1-77138-107-9 (bound)

    I. Title. II. Title: Mori no oku no ochakai e. English.

PZ7.M682Te 2015   j895.6'36   C2014-906946-4

Kids Can Press is a /©ΓUS™ Entertainment company

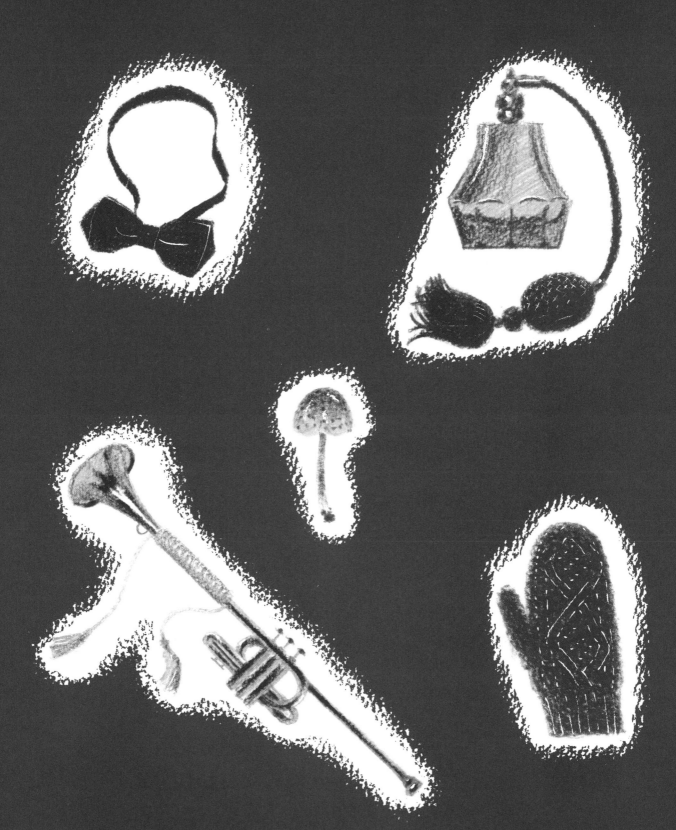